P9-BYB-613

When
I Wore My
Sailor Suit

Uri Shulevitz

FARRAR
STRAUS
GIROUX
NEW YORK

In memory of my mother

Copyright © 2009 by Uri Shulevitz

All rights reserved

Distributed in Canada by Douglas & McIntyre Ltd.

Color separations by Chroma Graphics PTE Ltd.

Printed and bound in the United States of America by Phoenix Color Corporation

Designed by Robbin Gourley

First edition, 2009

10   9   8   7   6   5   4   3   2   1

www.fsgkidsbooks.com

Library of Congress Cataloging-in-Publication Data

Shulevitz, Uri, date.

    When I wore my sailor suit / Uri Shulevitz. — 1st ed.

        p.   cm.

    Summary: A young child spends the day imagining himself to be a sailor on a grand
adventure.

        ISBN-13: 978-0-374-34749-9

        ISBN-10: 0-374-34749-2

        [1. Adventure and adventurers—Fiction.   2. Sailors—Fiction.   3. Imagination—Fiction.]
    I. Title.

PZ7.S5594 Whe 2009

[E]—dc22

                                            2008016187

When morning comes, I put on my sailor suit, my sailor hat, and my sailor whistle.

"Where to, sailor?" Mother asks.

"Today I sail on a ship," I announce.

"A journey requires provisions," she says, and puts an apple and a cookie in my little valise.

"Bon voyage, captain!" she says.

I give her my best sailor salute, I blow my sailor whistle, and I'm off.

A sailor's life isn't easy.
I must climb mountains to reach my destination.

After an arduous climb, I knock on the Mintzes' door.

My friend Mr. Mintz opens the door and says, "Well, hello, sailor. Come in."

"Today I sail on a ship," I declare.

"Today I sail to work," he says. "Bon voyage, captain." And he leaves.

On top of a dresser is a ship waiting for me, ready for departure.
Carefully, I take the ship down, put it gently on the floor,

and my journey begins.

I sail.
The seas are calm. The sun is shining.

The waves start to rise. They go higher and higher. A terrible storm comes up.
A sailor's life is dangerous. But a sailor must be brave!

Valiantly, I keep sailing.
When the storm realizes that I won't quit,
it quits.
The seas become calm again.

After a long voyage, I land on a sunny island.
I walk through luxurious vegetation. All is peaceful.

But the peace is disrupted by a strange *clump*, *clump*, *clump*.
I hide and watch.

Oh no! It is that horrible Malenostro Malevostro, pirate of one hundred seas!
He has one leg, one eye, one ear, and one arm,
and in his one arm he carries a rolled-up paper.

I stay hidden.
Malenostro Malevostro's clumping wakes three sleeping monkeys.
They are annoyed at having their afternoon nap disturbed
and begin pelting him with coconuts.

Malenostro Malevostro the famous pirate is so startled by the barrage of coconuts that he drops his paper and hops away as fast as he can.

I sneak out from my hiding place, snatch the paper, and run away.
When I'm safe, I unroll it.
I can't believe my eyes.
A treasure map!

I can't wait to go on a treasure hunt.
But what's that?
I feel someone is watching me.

Suddenly I'm back in the Mintzes' apartment.
I look around. I see no one in the room.

I try to resume my voyage. But I still feel that I'm being watched.
I look again.

Now I see.
It's the man in the picture on the wall.

I try to smile at him.
He does not smile back. He just stares at me sternly.

I try to ignore him and return to the ship, to sail away. But his gaze follows me.
I sail left. His eyes follow me left. I sail right. His eyes follow me right. I hide in a corner.
His eyes follow me there. I get angry. I blow my whistle as loud as I can.

Mr. Mintz's mother, Grandma Mintz, looks in from another room.
When she sees me, she smiles. The man pretends to smile, too.
As soon as she leaves, he stops smiling and glares at me.

I crawl under a table and hide behind the tablecloth.
Maybe he'll forget me.

I eat my apple and my cookie silently, and I wait.

At long last, I peek out.
As soon as he sees me, he looks at me severely.
He never leaves the wall, yet he always knows where I am.

I wait some more. Then, carefully, I crawl out from under the table.
Quietly, I put the ship back on top of the dresser, tiptoe out of the room,
and run home.

Days go by.
I think of the man in the picture.

I decide to return to the Mintzes' apartment.
This time I don't hide.
I walk over to the man in the picture and say,
"You can't leave this wall,
you can't leave this room,

but I can go far away on an exciting journey."